Shellica's Mermaid ADVENTURE

Jessica Slating
Illustrated by Ron Pence

Pacific Coast Creative Publishing, Los Angeles

Pacific Coast Creative Publishing
2816 Armacost Ave
Los Angeles, CA 90064

Manufactured in the United States.

ISBN: 978-0-9897415-6-9

Printed on acid free paper. Interior pages are Sustainable Forestry Initiative (SFI) certified. Meets all
ANSI standards for achrival quality paper.

My name is Shellica and I love to swim. I would swim all day long if I could.

One day, when I was swimming in our pool, Mom called out, "Shellica, if you don't get out of that pool, you're going to turn into a fish."

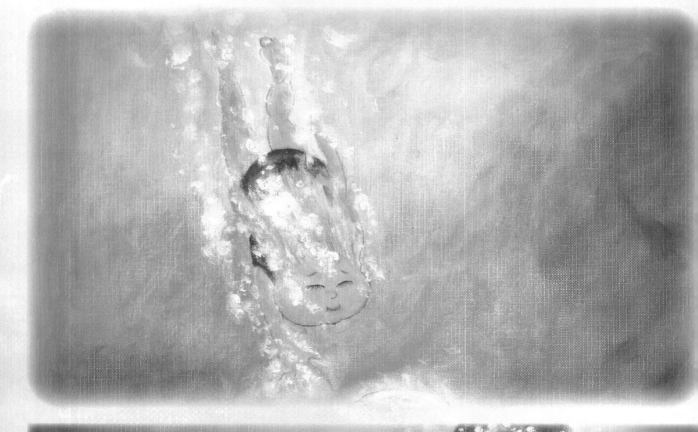

But I didn't listen to my mom. I wanted to dive to the bottom of the pool one more time. I love the cool and refreshing feeling of the water so much. I swam down as deep as I could go, and then pushed with my feet back up to the top of the water.

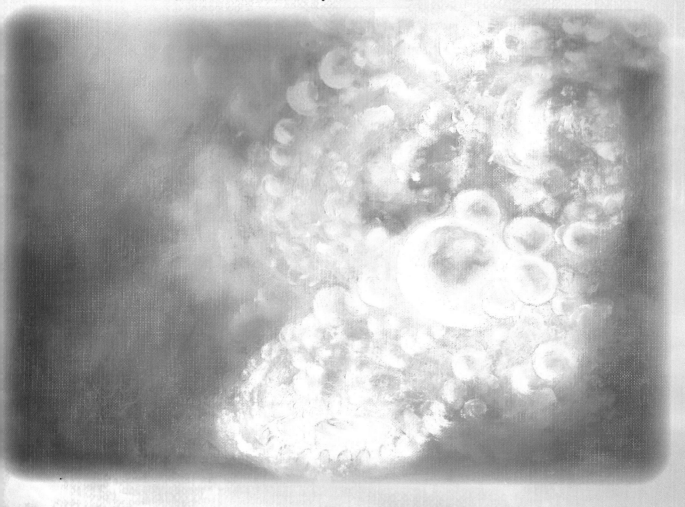

As I made my way to the top, I was swimming faster than ever before. I reached the ladder in no time and tried to climb out.

But then something funny happened...

I could not get my foot on the ladder. I looked down to see what was wrong and saw a big fish in the pool.

But it wasn't a fish...

It was me!

My legs had turned into a fish tail! "I'm a mermaid," I shouted happily. "Now I can swim all day long."

I splashed down in the water and swam around and around.

Mom came out again and shouted, "Shellica, this is the last time I'm going to tell you …"

"What in the world was that?" Mom exclaimed.

I popped my head out of the water and said,
"It's me!"

Mom said, "I told you if you didn't come out of that pool you'd turn into a fish. I told you so!"

But I was happy. I liked being a mermaid and couldn't wait to show all of my friends.

My friends came over and we swam and played in the water. They all thought it was so incredible that I was a mermaid!

We had fun for a long time until they didn't want to swim anymore. They wanted to go ride bikes and play at the park.

My friends helped me out of the pool so I could go with them. They dried off my mermaid tail so it would turn back into legs. But that didn't work. I was still a mermaid.

So my friends went to the park while I stayed at the pool.

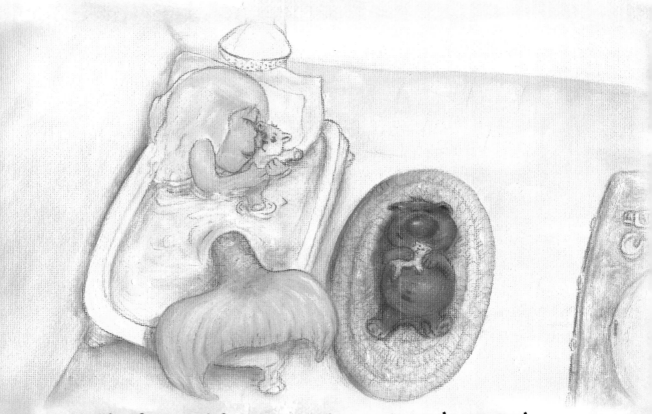

That night, I slept in the bathtub.

The next day, Mom dressed me in a long dress to cover my mermaid tail. She didn't want me to be too distracting in class.

Then she sent me to school in a wheelbarrow.

My mermaid tail got a lot of attention at school. No one was even listening to the teacher. A kid in my class even tripped over my tail and fell right into the science project.

It was hard to be at school, so I called my Mom and went home early.

The next day, my family and I went to the beach. It was fun to jump in and out of the waves. I learned I could stay underwater for so long and explore all the beautiful sea life. I was really enjoying myself!

A school of fish swam up to me and we all played by swimming in a circle. They swam faster and faster - and we were suddenly a long way from shore.

I saw my family far away on the beach and was afraid to go further out to sea. "HELP-HELP!" I cried.

My Dad came to the rescue, scooped me up, and
we all went home.

The next day, when I woke up, I was still a mermaid. How was I going to go to school or play with my friends? I thought I should have changed back into myself by now. I felt sad.

Mom thought up ways to get me help. First, she took me to the pediatrician.

The pediatrician took my temperature and measured me. Then she told me: "Take some of this medicine and you should be back to normal in no time." But that didn't work.

Next, we visited the veterinarian.

The veterinarian took some x-rays and looked in my ears. Then, he gave me a shot in my tail. That didn't work either.

Then, we drove to the zoo for help. The zoologist gladly offered, "I want to keep Shellica in the zoo and study her." Mom quickly picked me up and rushed us right out the door.

After that, my parents took me to the people at Ocean World; they might know what to do.

A marine biologist there happily said, "Shellica would be perfect in our Ocean Show!" Ugh! I didn't want to be in a fish show. I just wanted to turn back to my normal self.
I felt really sad.

Finally, we went to Grandma's house. Grandma told me, "Shellica, all you need to do is listen to your mother." That sounded so easy, but I try all the time and it's so hard.

That night, Mom told me to eat my vegetables at dinner. I didn't want to.

Mom told me not to tease my sister, but my sister was being so mean.

Mom told me to clean my room, but I thought it looked good the way it was.

Just then, I remembered what Grandma said ...

So I cleaned my room,

played with my sister...

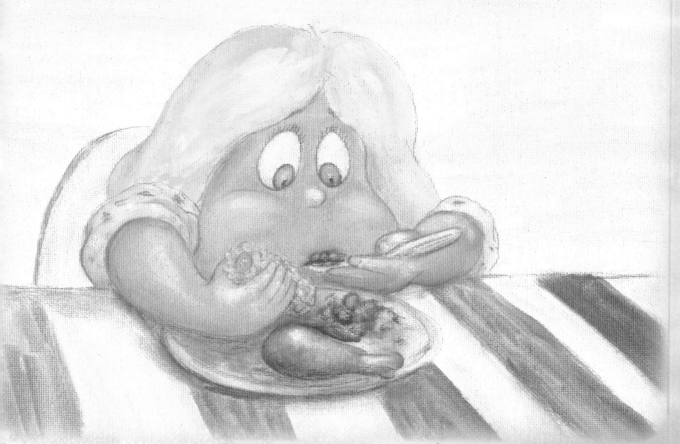

and ate my vegetables
(that were very cold now).

Then I went to my bed in the bathtub.

The next morning when I woke up, something was different. I could wiggle my toes ... YAY!

My fish tail was gone. I was me again!
Grandma was right; all I ever had to do was
listen to my Mom.

I'll always love to swim, but I like being myself
even more.

That night, my sister and I didn't want to go to bed. Mom told us, "You better get into bed before midnight or you'll turn into pumpkins!"

So this time I listened!